AMERICAN
ADVENTURES

★ ★ ★

WESTWARD JOURNEYS

The Oklahoma Land Run
The Oregon Trail

Grateful acknowledgment is made to the following for permission to reprint previously published material:

Minnow and Rose: An Oregon Trail Story by Judy Young, illustrated by Bill Farnsworth. Text copyright © 2009 by Judy Young. Illustrations copyright © 2009 by Bill Farnsworth. Originally published by Sleeping Bear Press, 2009.

Pappy's Handkerchief by Devin Scillian, illustrated by Chris Ellison. Text copyright © 2007 by Devin Scillian. Illustrations copyright © 2007 by Chris Ellison. Originally published by Sleeping Bear Press, 2007.

A Book for Black-Eyed Susan by Judy Young, illustrated by Doris Ettlinger. Text copyright © 2011 by Judy Young. Illustrations copyright © 2011 by Doris Ettlinger. Originally published by Sleeping Bear Press, 2011.

—〜〜—

Sleeping Bear Press™

315 E. Eisenhower Parkway, Ste. 200
Ann Arbor, MI 48108
www.sleepingbearpress.com

Printed and bound in the United States.

10 9 8 7 6 5 4 3 2 1

Library of Congress Cataloging-in-Publication Data • Young, Judy. • Westward journeys / written by Judy Young, Devin Scillian; • illustrated by Bill Farnsworth, Chris Ellison, Doris Ettlinger. • v. cm. – (American adventures) • Summary: "Westward Journeys contains stories focusing on the American westward expansion. Minnow and Rose: a girl on the Oregon Trail meets a native girl. Pappy's Handkerchief: an African-American family during the Oklahoma Land Run. A Book for Black-Eyed Susan: a girl facing tragedy on the Oregon Trail"– Provided by publisher. • Contents: Minnow and Rose: an Oregon Trail story — Pappy's handkerchief — A book for Black-eyed Susan. • ISBN 978-1-58536-860-0 • [1. Frontier and pioneer life– Fiction. 2. Wagon trains–Fiction. 3. African Americans–Fiction. 4. Oregon National Historic Trail–Fiction. 5. Oklahoma–History–Land Rush, 1889–Fiction. 6. West (U.S.)–History–19th century–Fiction.] • I. Scillian, Devin. II. Farnsworth, Bill, illustrator. III. Ellison, Chris, illustrator. IV. Ettlinger, Doris, illustrator. V. Title. • PZ7.Y8664Wes 2014 • [Fic]–dc23 • 2012046804

TABLE OF CONTENTS

Minnow and Rose

THE OREGON TRAIL

Judy Young

Illustrated by Bill Farnsworth

Her name was Girl-Who-Comes-With-Berries, but everyone called her Minnow.

She was supposed to be born when heat waves in the grasses, but came early during days of juicy berries. Minnow was small even though she had seen ten seasons of berry picking, but she could swim like a fish. She was constantly thinking of ways to get in the water. When sent to pick berries, Minnow often crawled through the prickly branches and slipped into the river that ran alongside the village. But today she wanted to float down the rapids.

"Can I go to the crossing spot?" Minnow asked. "There are lots of berries to pick there."

"Yes, but be careful," said her mother.

Minnow grabbed a basket.

Minnow followed the river upstream and

got busy picking. Suddenly, she became aware of noises. They were different from the river's song.

Peeking through the leaves, she saw covered wagons forming a circle on the other side of the river. Minnow knew what that meant. Strangers were coming across the prairie again!

Rose walked beside the wagon, wishing something exciting would happen. For over a month they had traveled across the never-ending prairie. Every day was the same. When the horn blew at five, they got up, ate, packed, and moved on.

Today seemed no different than the others. But in mid-morning the wagon train started to circle up.

"Why are we stopping?" Rose asked.

"There's a river ahead," said Pa. "We'll set up camp and cross tomorrow."

"Good," said Ma. "We need to wash. Look at Rose's hair!"

Rose had been named for her shocking red hair. Now, like everything else, it was covered with dust kicked up by the oxen.

"I'll fetch some water," Rose said, grabbing a bucket.

The river rushed deep and fast. Rose walked downstream. Soon the rapids slowed to a still pool. There, Rose found a wonderful surprise. Big, juicy berries!

Rose crawled through the thorny branches, putting berries in her bucket until she reached the water's edge. She stuck her head into the river and her hair returned to its coppery color. When she raised her head, she heard noises. It sounded like camp, but it was coming from the other side of the river.

Rose peered across. There was a camp. But there were no covered wagons in this camp. Across the river were teepees. Rose knew what that meant. Indians!

"I must tell Father about the wagons!" Minnow thought.

Minnow put her basket into the rushing water and jumped in. As she floated alongside the basket, she saw a girl running along the bank. Minnow had never seen a girl like this one. Her hair was the color of the setting sun. The girl stopped and looked down at Minnow. Their eyes met. The red-haired girl had eyes like the summer sky.

Rose had been running as fast as she could, following the river upstream. She needed to tell Pa about the teepees. Suddenly, something strange caught her eye. She stopped and stared at the water. A basket floated down the river. But that wasn't all. Alongside the basket was a girl with pitch-black hair. The girl in the river had eyes as dark as a moonless night.

Minnow reached her village and ran to her father. "Wagons like the ones that came last year are at the crossing!" she said excitedly.

"We should go meet them," Father said. "Perhaps they need our help to cross the river."

As the men gathered and mounted their horses, Father told Minnow to go home. But Minnow wanted to see the red-haired girl again.

"It would show you come in friendship if a child came with you, Father," she said. Then, she added, "I am the one who saw them first."

Father looked sternly at Minnow but lifted her onto the back of his horse. "When we get there, stay on the horse," he commanded.

Minnow's father led the way to the crossing spot. The horses plunged into the water and swam across. A group of men stood near the wagons, watching them arrive.

Women and children peeked out from behind the wagons' dusty covers. As Father got off the horse, Minnow looked carefully for the girl with red hair.

"Stay in the wagon," Pa told Rose.

Rose leaned out over the wagon seat to watch. One horse had two riders, a man with a small girl sitting behind him. Rose looked carefully. It was the girl from the river.

Minnow slipped off the horse and walked toward the wagon. The red-haired girl carefully climbed down. They both stood and looked at each other. Then, the red-haired girl grabbed a handful of berries from the bucket. She offered the juicy fruit to Minnow.

Minnow took the berries, popped them in her mouth, and smiled. "Minnow," she said, pointing to herself. Then she held up a long black braid. With her other hand, Minnow pointed at the girl's bright red hair.

The red-haired girl stepped back nervously. Minnow smiled and pointed to herself again. "Minnow," she repeated.

The red-haired girl smiled back. "Rose," she answered, placing her hand on her chest. "I'm Rose."

Minnow repeated the name, "Rose."

Suddenly, a man's loud voice called out harshly. Quick as lightning, Minnow raced back to her scolding father and climbed up onto the horse.

Minnow's father had offered to help the pioneers cross the river in exchange for tools, and the pioneers had accepted. Early the next morning the two groups met at the crossing spot.

One by one, each wagon was unloaded and the wheels taken off. The empty wagon was tied to a raft and reloaded. Using ropes, a team of oxen on the other side pulled the raft across the water. Then everything was removed from the wagon again. The empty wagon was taken off the raft and the wheels put back on. One last time, it was reloaded as the oxen were yoked.

As Rose waited for her family's turn, she kept a lookout for Minnow.

"Come along, Rose," said Pa. "We're next."

"Did you see her, Pa?" Rose asked.

"No," Pa answered. "Maybe you'll see her tonight. I have to take tools to their village to pay them for helping us. You can come with me."

Rose climbed up on the wagon seat beside Pa. The raft was slowly pulled into the water. It wobbled and tipped, but Rose didn't notice. She was too busy searching the far bank. The raft was about halfway across when Rose spotted Minnow, hiding in some berry bushes.

Rose stood up to wave. The raft tipped to one side. Before Pa could grab her, Rose fell into the rushing river.

Minnow had wanted to watch the wagons cross the river, but her father said, "No, you did not mind me yesterday."

Minnow watched the men ride away from her village, but then she followed them to the crossing spot. She hid in the berry bushes and looked for Rose.

At last Minnow spotted her, sitting on the seat of a wagon tied to a raft. As the raft moved toward the middle of the river, she saw Rose stand up to wave.

Suddenly, the raft lurched. Minnow watched Rose fly from the wagon seat and disappear into the water.

It all happened so fast, Rose didn't even have time to take a breath!

Panicking, she kicked and flailed her arms but the strong rapids tossed her around and the weight of her dress pulled her down.

Suddenly, something grabbed hold of her hair. Rose tried to get away, but she couldn't. The grasp was too tight and the water too powerful. Soon she was too tired to fight.

Minnow watched the long red hair disappear under the water. Quickly, she jumped in the river, dove under like an otter, and grabbed at the swirling hair. She caught a big bunch in her hand and hung on tight. Minnow tried to kick back up to the surface, but Rose fought her as much as the strong rapids did.

Just when Minnow thought she could hold her breath no longer, Rose's body went limp. Keeping a firm grip on Rose's hair, Minnow kicked with all her might and dragged Rose's head above the rippling currents.

Rose coughed and gasped for breath but Minnow held her tight. Together the two girls bobbed downstream until the fast-moving waters poured into the calm pool. Minnow kicked toward the bank until they

could touch bottom.

Then the two girls crawled out and lay totally exhausted under the low branches of the berry bushes.

Everyone on the riverbank ran downstream, watching Minnow pull Rose to safety. They carried the two girls back to the crossing. Rose's worried family, who had helplessly watched from the middle of

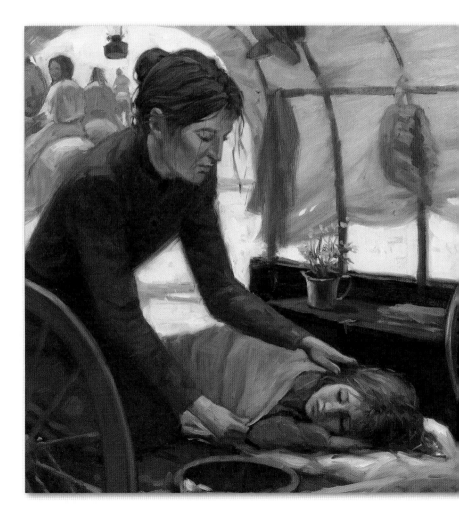

the river, had just reached the far side.

Soon Rose lay snug and dry, sleeping in her wagon and Minnow rode back home, snuggled against the back of her father.

When Rose awoke later, her first thoughts were of Minnow. She wanted to give her something, not only for saving her life, but to offer in friendship. Mother baked a berry cobbler for her to take to the village but Rose wanted something more. Something only she could give.

As she brushed her hair, Rose knew what it would be. She gathered bundles of dried grass. She folded and braided the grasses, then neatly stitched some colorful scraps of material around them.

"Perfect," she thought, "except for one last part."

Minnow was the hero of her village. She enjoyed the attention but her thoughts kept turning to Rose. They had only just met, yet after what happened at the river she felt a strong bond with the red-haired girl.

Minnow wanted to give Rose something of herself. She slipped away to the quiet of the river to think about it.

That evening Minnow and Rose sat side by side. A big dish of cobbler sat in front of them. Smiles glowed on their faces and in their hands were gifts of friendship.

FROM THE AUTHOR,
Judy Young

In writing *Minnow and Rose*, I not only wanted to show a glimpse of life on the trail, but also the positive relationship that often existed between the pioneers and the Native Americans. During the early days of the Oregon Trail, encounters between the two cultures were often business trans-actions, bartering goods such as tools, livestock, food, and other merchandise for services. One service frequently document-ed was help at river crossings.

Today, we easily zoom across rivers on bridges, but to the pioneers river crossings were laborious and dangerous. Wagon trains often took several days to cross just one river. Sometimes wagons toppled over and pioneers not only lost their belongings, but also their lives. In 1857 at least 37 people drowned crossing the Green River in present-day Wyoming. There are also documented accounts of Native Americans saving pioneers from drowning.

I also wanted *Minnow and Rose* to illustrate that people are people no matter what cultures they come from. People are universally inquisitive about others and curious about their differences, but overall they want to make friends and be accepted.

Pappy's
Handkerchief

THE OKLAHOMA LAND RUN

Devin Scillian
Illustrated by Chris Ellison

March 25, 1889 - Baltimore, Maryland

The icy air smelled like salt and as the fishermen laid out the fish from their nets, large snowflakes began to land on the dark green waves off the Baltimore pier. As I did every day, I ran from home at lunchtime to help my father in our fish stall. But with the weather getting worse and a small day's catch from the fishermen, there were few takers for the goods on my father's table. Still, I cried out to the passersby as always.

"Codfish! Bluefish! Fresh today!

Clams and oysters fresh from the bay!"

Mrs. Wayburn came by, of course, for the clams to put in the soup she served in her tavern. And Mr. Sanders purchased some salt cod that my father pulled from the old oak barrel. But as the sky over the harbor darkened, my father counted the few coins in his change purse. He always hoped for enough to buy some beef or maybe even a chicken. But dinner tonight would again be the fish that we didn't sell. And I had never seen my father more sad as he closed down the fish stall for the evening.

We walked past the other stalls run by Negro families like ours, and then moved into the wharf where the white fishmongers had their stalls. They were a little busier, but not much. We walked the twelve blocks to our worn row house on Woolfolk Street, the cobblestones quickly disappearing beneath the snow. Usually we talked of the stall, or of the neighbors. But this night my father spoke not a word until we stood outside the entrance to Cook's General Store. As usual, there was a group of men from our neighborhood standing beneath the awning, arguing and talking about this and that. My father said nothing, but he listened.

"Oklahoma? That's Indian Territory. You go out there, you gonna git killed. And even if you don't, ain't nobody gonna give you no farm. That's crazy." It was Rupert Johnson talking in his deep voice. He was pointing in the face of Liberty Grosjean. Liberty could read and he often brought a newspaper to Cook's to tell what was happening in the world beyond our Baltimore row houses.

Oliver Burnett joined in. "You know that right, Liberty. Ain't nobody gonna give a farm away to a Negro. Simple as that." The other men clicked their tongues and nodded their heads in agreement.

"It says right here any American can stake a claim. You wait at the territory line. They'll fire a cannon and it's first come, first served. You've only got to promise to farm the land for five years and it's yours, absolutely free."

The crowd of men couldn't believe it, and they threw up their hands at Liberty and started to walk away. My father was listening to every word. And as the crowd moved away from Liberty, my father drew closer to him.

"Liberty, what's this you say? Where does a man go to get a free farm?"

"It's a long way, Ephraim. But this says the federal government is going to open up the Oklahoma Territory in a few weeks and let folks stake a claim. There's two million acres out there and you can have 160 of them."

"When does this happen?" my father asked.

"They're gonna fire the cannon at noon on April 22," said Liberty.

"But that's just a month from now!" said my father.

"I know," said Liberty. "I'm packing tonight and I'll be on the way in just a few days."

"You're really going?" my father asked. Liberty was young, just a few years older than me. But because he had been to school and could read, he had the respect of everyone in the neighborhood.

"Ephraim," said Liberty. "Slavery is over, and we're free now. But in America a man isn't really free until he owns the land he lives on. That's true for white folks and black folks alike. A chance like this comes once in a lifetime if you're lucky."

"Moses, you run on home for supper. I'll be right behind you." I did as I was told, but I kept looking back and watching my father talking with Liberty, and I could tell my father was making plans.

I walked into the small house that was hardly big enough for our family. My mother was changing the diaper of my baby brother, Noah. My other brother, James, was playing a game with my sisters, Virginia and Lacy. Pappy and Granny, my grandfather and grandmother, were sorting through a sack of small apples. I handed my mother the fish for dinner and I asked, "Momma, where's Oklahoma?"

She waved a hand at me. "I've no idea. Out west somewhere." But before the evening was out, Momma would know where Oklahoma was.

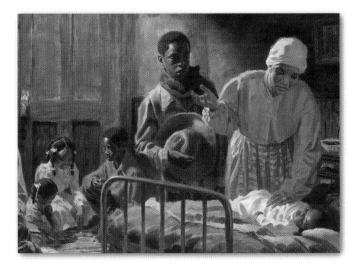

As soon as my father came home he talked quietly with Pappy. I could see old Pappy's eyebrows moving up and down. Pappy grew up as a slave on a peanut farm in Virginia. He had always dreamed of farming his own land, but when slavery ended, Pappy, Granny, and my father had their freedom, but little else. They figured they might find work in a city like Baltimore, and as they learned the fish trade, the dreams of a farm drifted farther and farther away.

As my brothers and sisters and I lay in our beds, the light from the lantern glowed late into the evening and the talk between my parents and grandparents went on and on.

And the next morning my father announced that we were moving to Oklahoma.

Most of our neighbors thought we were foolish. But there was almost no time to think about it. Pa needed to sell the fish stall. Pa's plan, suggested by Liberty, was to raise enough money to buy train tickets to Kansas City where we would buy a covered wagon and two horses to take us to Indian Territory. But when Pa and Pappy came home their faces were long. The only people interested in buying the stall wanted to pay for it over time. But our family needed the money now.

My parents and grandparents sold whatever they could—Granny's handmade lace tablecloths, most of my father's fish knives, Pappy's horn-handled cane, and even my parents' wedding rings. But it wasn't enough, and we were running out of time if we expected to be at the starting line when the cannon was fired.

And so it was a shock when Pa came in and rousted us from our beds and told us it was time to leave. He and Pappy had found a taker for the fish stall, a new arrival in Baltimore who had no money. But in return for the stall, he was willing to trade the one thing he did have: a wagon and two horses. And we were leaving right away!

"But Ephraim," said my mother, "how will we ever find our way? Can you find Indian Territory?"

"No," said my father. "But I know someone who can." At that moment, Liberty Grosjean appeared at the door with a huge sack on his back. In exchange for a ride to Oklahoma, Liberty would make sure we got there on time.

So with everything we could possibly pack loaded into the wagon, the ten of us pulled away from our row house just as the sun was beginning to redden the eastern horizon behind us. And soon the buildings of Baltimore were long gone.

I sat between Pa and Liberty on the front wagon seat. As my father gently called to the horses, Rumble and Maybelle, Liberty read his notes, watched the sun, and scribbled into a small brown book.

We rode for so many days. We rode through an ice storm in the Cumberland Mountains. It rained like I had never seen in West Virginia, and we nearly lost Maybelle in a flooded river in Kentucky. At night we made camp, often with other families making the same westward journey. We found that there were many Negro families headed for Oklahoma, people just like us who had heard that any American could stake a

claim. We traded stories and supplies, songs and directions. At night Pappy would unhitch Rumble and give me a ride on his smooth back. And Liberty was teaching Pa to read by the light of the campfire.

We occasionally saw signs of trouble. A few times, white riders came by telling us to go home. They said the rules had changed and Negroes weren't allowed in the land run,

but Liberty knew they were lying. One night in Tennessee, a wildcat frightened Ma half to death. We fell three days behind in Arkansas because we got lost. And most concerning, Noah was sick with fever for nearly a week. But we knew we were getting closer and closer because the trails were getting very crowded with settlers. Liberty and Pa began to worry about whether there would be enough land for everyone.

On Saturday, April 20, we arrived at a camp in Indian Territory near a town called Kingfisher. We had arrived just in time. We were running low on food. The trip had been hard on Maybelle and she was beginning to limp. And while little Noah was feeling better, the fever had now moved on to Pappy. He lay in the back of the wagon and told us not to worry and that he would be ready for Monday morning.

There were people and horses and wagons and mules everywhere, camped along a line of white stakes stretching across the flat Oklahoma plains. The horizon had never seemed so far away. Soldiers rode between the campfires explaining the rules for the run and warning us about straying across the boundary line too soon. And sure enough, every so often, soldiers would ride in from the boundary with a cheater under arrest.

The next night, Sunday, there were huge bonfires up and down the line of settlers. People sang songs into the clear night. We made camp with lots of other Negro families. The men talked excitedly about the best way to stake a claim. Several of the men had decided that the only way to get a claim was to sneak across the line late at night.

"Look at all these folks," said one. "And there's railroad cars bringing more every couple of hours. There ain't gonna be nothing left by the time they let the Negroes in."

"Not one acre," said another. "If we don't sneak in there tonight, we might as well turn around and go home."

Lots of men nodded in agreement, but Liberty spoke up. "No. You see what's happening to the Sooners. They're being arrested and sent away. That's the best way to end up with nothing. And no one said anything about Negroes going in last. We're not

Negroes here. We're Americans. We go in same as everyone else."

Several men stood to argue, but Liberty looked to my father. "Ephraim, you got any plans to turn around and go home?"

"I am home," said my father. And a silence fell on all of us as we stared into the crackling fire. I looked up and realized I had never seen a sky so full of stars. And I loved the feeling that this was our home forever.

Monday, April 22, 1889, dawned with a blazing sunshine as beautiful a spring day as there ever was. Even more settlers had arrived overnight and the crowd of home-steaders now stretched as far as I could see. No one had slept much and now there was so much excitement in the air I could barely breathe. But Ma was hollering for Pa to come to the back of the wagon.

I followed Pa and we arrived to find my mother with her head in her hands. Pappy was not doing well. That was bad enough. But now Liberty, too, was covered in shiny sweat and shaking with fever.

My mother looked at my father. "Well," said Pa, "if we can just get to our claim . . ."

"Then what?" asked my mother. "Then what? We have nothing, Ephraim. There will be no house. There will be no well, no barn, no stove, no bed waiting for us. There's no doctor to call. We'll have nothing but a piece of dirt."

Granny was quietly crying, caressing Pappy's tired, weathered face. All around us, wagons and horses were moving closer to the line. I saw so many different kinds of people. They were white and black, wealthy and poor, young and old. Pa knew that Ma was right. But he did the only thing he could do.

He told us all to hang on because the ride was going to be fast and bumpy.

For the next few hours, every settler had an eye on the sky. As the sun climbed toward high noon, Pa guided our wagon toward the line. He reached under the buckboard and handed Liberty's long rifle to me.

"It ain't loaded," he said. "But no one else has to know that."

Granny made sure Pappy and Liberty were low in the wagon and pulled James, Virginia, and Lacy close to her. Ma held Noah tightly in her arms. And we waited.

Suddenly, a cannon fired from the east, a BOOM that sent half the horses rearing back on their hind legs. But in a huge cloud of dust, the swarm of settlers dashed into the land that looked so golden and so precious from our camps. Those on single horses raced way out in front and quickly disappeared on the far horizon. The very first wagons across the line only had to travel a few hundred yards to stake claims on the first acres up for grabs. But they were nearly run over as they tried to stop on their new homestead with so many others having to charge through to stake the next claim.

We had to wait a few minutes for the wagons in front of us to get on their way, but finally Rumble and Maybelle crossed the

line amid the whoops and hollers of the thousands of settlers around us. The land before us finally opened up and we were dashing along with a stiff Oklahoma wind in our faces. But long gone were the smooth trails of well-traveled country. Indian Territory was covered in deep ruts and culverts and our wagon began to bounce furiously across the ditches. Liberty's head hit hard on the floor of the wagon, and James and Lacy were crying because they were so afraid.

The deep grass hid the dry creek bed ahead of us. We never saw it, and neither did Maybelle as she stumbled forward on her bad leg and lost her footing. She tumbled down and the wagon jerked violently to her side. Pa tried to pull back on Rumble's rein, but suddenly the front wheel bounced down into the ditch and as Maybelle fell, the wagon bounced hard into the air and smashed back to the ground. Pa and I flew off the buckboard and into the grass. Rumble was down, too, and both horses whinnied in pain.

While Pa made sure everyone was okay, I stared at our disaster. Our front wagon wheel was solidly lodged in the ditch. And Maybelle's reins were trapped beneath it, leaving her hopelessly jerking her head against the weight of the wagon. Pa jumped into the ditch and grabbed the forward corner of the wagon. He let out a groan and suddenly the wagon lifted just enough for Maybelle to free her rein. But Pa slipped as the weight of the wagon came crashing back down into the creek bed and right onto his left leg. The snap of my father's leg breaking filled the air just ahead of his painful scream.

Ma had to empty everyone from the wagon and it still took her, Granny, and me to pull the wagon off my father. And with wagons, riders, and even runners racing by, our

very dreams lay broken and beaten in a dry
Oklahoma creek bed.

It was chaos. My brothers and sisters were
crying. My mother was dazed. Granny was
trying to catch her breath, and I honestly
wasn't sure Liberty was alive.

But Pappy, looking weak, let out a loud
groan. He raised himself from the grass and
looked out across the Oklahoma plain and
turned to me.

"Moses," he said. "It's up to you."

I had no idea what he meant. But he reached
into his pocket and drew out a white handkerchief.

"You take Rumble," he said. "You ride like
the wind, as far and as fast as you can. And
when you find our farm, you bury this
handkerchief in the ground and you claim
it as ours."

I expected someone to protest. But as I looked to my father, I could see that he was already trying to reach over to unharness Rumble.

Rumble was angry enough over the accident that he needed no coaxing from me to run. It was all I could do to hold on to his mane. He flew like a blur across the countryside, passing wagon and rider alike. I have no idea how long he ran or how many miles we galloped. We rode past so many stakes in the ground, so many claims that were taken, some obviously taken days ago by Sooners.

But with sweat steaming off his neck and a lather foaming at his mouth, Rumble raced two other riders along a flowing creek. I knew water could mean everything for a farm, so I followed every turn and bend in the water and at last could see no stakes in the ground. I pulled Rumble to a stop and pulled from my back pocket the only possession I had. I plunged Pappy's handkerchief in the ground just as the sun was beginning to set in the western sky.

Was it mine? Was this our farm? Rumble began to drink from the creek and I sat down and wondered what to do next. I didn't even know where I was! But just before nightfall, two U.S. marshals made their way along the creek, taking stock of the claims.

"Is this your claim, son?" one of them asked me.

My voice cracked a little, but I said, "Yes, yes it is."

They looked at each other. One said, "You've got to be eighteen to make a claim, son. Are you eighteen?"

I wasn't eighteen. But what was I supposed to say? Miles away, my family lay broken and sick, counting on me. I bit my lip and looked at the marshals.

The first one smiled, raised a small notebook and asked, "What's your name, son? Nice claim you got here."

Pa was right. We were home.

It would be several days before I would see my family. A doctor had set Pa's leg and he was going to be fine. Liberty's fever had finally broken, and he was already drawing up a farm plan in his notebook. Even Maybelle was pulling through.

—m—

Sadly, Pappy would never get to see the farm he had dreamed of since his days as a slave peanut picker. But long after our house and barn had been built, and long after the first stalks of corn popped through the red soil, Pappy's handkerchief continued to wave in the ever-present Oklahoma breeze.

FROM THE AUTHOR,
Devin Scillian

The day of April 22, 1889, began with an empty plain in Oklahoma. By nightfall, homesteads stretched to the horizon, and Oklahoma City and Guthrie had suddenly sprung to life, each with an instant population of 10,000 people.

The history of Oklahoma is terribly complicated. Opening up the Oklahoma Territory for settlers meant, of course, taking the land away from Native Americans who endured unspeakable hardships. At the same time, it allowed others the chance at a new life.

While we talk about the Oklahoma Land Run, there were actually five different runs between 1889 and 1895. *Pappy's Handkerchief* isn't about any one family or even one land run. The story is a medley of the struggles and experiences of thousands of families who journeyed west to live as pioneers on the prairie. They were way out on a limb, and the fruit they harvested is alive in the spirit of Oklahoma today.

A Book for Black-Eyed Susan

THE OREGON TRAIL

Judy Young
Illustrated by Doris Ettlinger

It was still dark when Cora awoke. She looked across the prairie and saw her family's wagon glowing with lantern light. Yesterday Pa pulled their wagon away from where the others circled for the night, but told ten-year-old Cora to stay with Uncle Lee.

Cora ran through the tall grasses until she reached her wagon. Aunt Alma was inside holding a baby. Pa sat leaning against the wagon wheel, his head in his hands. Something was wrong.

"Where's Ma?" Cora could barely squeak out the words.

When Pa lifted his head, the lantern light fell across his face. Tears rolled down his cheeks. All he could do was shake his head and pull Cora tight to his chest.

When the sun lightened the sky, Cora and Pa stood side by side on a small hill. The others had already left the gravesite to get ready to move on.

"What about the baby?" Cora asked.

"Aunt Alma can take care of her," said Pa.

It was soon time to leave. Cora sat in the back of their wagon. Through her tears, she watched the wooden cross on the hill become smaller and smaller until it disappeared. Then, she lay down and cried herself to sleep.

The wagon bumped and jiggled across the prairie. Cora awoke when she felt its movement stop at noon. She climbed out and walked slowly to Aunt Alma's and Uncle Lee's wagon.

"Do you want to hold her?" Aunt Alma asked.

Cora sat down and Aunt Alma placed the baby in her arms. As Cora softly stroked the tassel of yellow hair on her sister's head, the baby opened her eyes. They were pitch-black.

That evening, Pa and Cora sat in front of the fire. They could hear Aunt Alma singing quietly to the baby.

"Pa," Cora said. "I have a good name for the baby."

"What?" Pa asked.

"Susan," Cora said. "She reminds me of black-eyed Susans."

"That's a beautiful name," Pa said. "Your ma would like that name, too."

"They were Ma's favorite flowers," said Cora, remembering how she picked handfuls along the trail for her mother.

The days rolled on just as the wagon train did. Cora helped Aunt Alma with Susan as much as possible. But one stormy day, Cora sat alone in her own wagon. As rain pelted on the canvas, she pulled out her mother's sewing box.

Thumbing through the scraps, there were many pieces she recognized. A piece from her Gramma's apron, one from Grampa's shirt, and another from Ma's favorite dress. Cora thought of the house they had left in Missouri. Gramma on the porch, Grampa leading the mules to the barn. She thought about Ma. Susan would never know any of them. She wouldn't even remember the trip to Oregon. Suddenly, Cora had an idea.

Cora took the scissors and cut squares, triangles, and rectangles from the scraps. She arranged the shapes on the largest square, threaded a needle, and started sewing. When she was done, she held up the square and smiled, remembering the farmhouse back in Missouri.

Across the prairie, Cora worked on different squares. One had a covered wagon. Another, a campfire with the cooking spider. Some had pictures of animals Cora saw along the way. Prairie dogs peeking from their holes, buffalo, a coyote, a hawk. There was a square with the strangely shaped cliff called Chimney Rock. Another showing a wagon crossing a river, and then mountains rising blue in the distance.

One evening Pa came to Cora. His face was sad, his eyes tired. He put his arm around Cora and without talking they walked away from the wagons. At last Pa broke the silence.

"I've asked Aunt Alma and Uncle Lee to raise Susan," he said.

"No!" Cora stopped, turning to face her father. "I can take care of her."

"You're too young," Pa said, "and a baby needs a mother."

"But they're going to California," Cora argued. "We'll never see her again."

"Yes, I know. We've gone through South Pass and tomorrow the train will divide up," Pa said. He sighed and shook his head. "This isn't the way I want things to be, Cora, but it will be best for Susan."

Cora turned and ran as hard as she could. Away from Pa, away from the wagons, away from the baby. Finally exhausted, she dropped into the grasses and stared back east, toward her home a thousand miles away.

Cora knew, deep down, Pa was trying to do what was best. Aunt Alma was already being a good mother to Susan. But Cora didn't know if she could stand watching them leave with Susan tomorrow. Suddenly, she jumped up.

"Tomorrow!" she said, "I've only got 'til tomorrow!"

Cora raced back to the wagon and grabbed the sewing box. She carefully embroidered a square until it was dotted with black-eyed Susans. Then she took all the other squares she had made and stitched them together. She smiled as she leafed through them. It would be Susan's first book.

The next morning Cora rushed to Aunt Alma's wagon. Susan was sleeping. Cora gave her a good-bye kiss on the forehead and turned to Aunt Alma. She wanted to tell Aunt Alma about the book, but all she could do was push the cloth pages into her aunt's hands. Aunt Alma looked at each page and then wrapped her arms around Cora.

"I promise when Susan gets older, I'll give her this book, and tell her the story about how she crossed the prairie," Aunt Alma said. "And that she has a sister named Cora who loves her very much."

The wagon train divided. Cora and Pa moved on, crossing the high plains desert, then into the mountains, and weeks later finally reaching Oregon Territory. Soon Pa had built a home, and then a farm. A town grew up and a school was built.

Months passed into years. Cora did well in her studies and six years after she left Missouri, she took a test to become a teacher. It wasn't long before she was offered a position. A minister and his wife would journey south to open a new church and she would go with them to teach school.

"We have a few slates, but no books," the minister said as he showed Cora the schoolhouse. "We've asked the students to bring any they have from home."

"I've brought my old readers," Cora replied, setting them on the desk beside the slates. She also pulled out a ledger, a bottle of ink, and a pen. When the children arrived she asked them to line up in front of her desk.

"What's your name?" Cora asked the first child. She carefully dipped her pen and wrote his name in her ledger. She did the same with two more boys.

The next child stood in front of her desk. "And your name?" Cora asked, looking up from the ledger.

"My name is Susan, and I have a book."

FROM THE AUTHOR,
Judy Young

Traveling on the Oregon Trail was not easy for the pioneers. There were many physical hardships, but there were emotional hardships as well. One that almost everyone faced was separation.

From their first steps west, the pioneers were separated from loved ones that stayed behind. Along the way, death also separated families and friends. Approximately one in seventeen died during the journey from illness, accidents, or in childbirth. Many children lost one parent, some both. It was up to other family members, friends, or even strangers to take care of surviving children, and sometimes siblings were divided among several families.

Near South Pass in what is currently southwestern Wyoming, the trail divided, separating those who had traveled together for more than 900 miles. Some took the California Trail with dreams of finding gold in that new state. Others continued traveling on the Oregon Trail toward the good farmland in Oregon Territory.

When writing historical fiction, research is used to support imagination so all that happens in the story could have happened, even if it didn't in reality. In *A Book for Black-Eyed Susan*, Cora and her family are entirely fictitious, but the events that happened to them were all possible.

Judy Young is an award-winning author of children's fiction, nonfiction, and poetry. Her other books include *The Lucky Star* (2009 *Storytelling World* Honor Award) and *Tuki and Moka: A Tale of Two Tamarins*. Judy lives near Springfield, Missouri.

Bill Farnsworth is a graduate of the Ringling School of Art and Design. He has created paintings for magazines, advertisements, children's books, and fine art commissions. His numerous book awards include a Teachers' Choice Award. Bill lives in Florida.

Devin Scillian is an award-winning author and Emmy award-winning broadcast journalist. His children's books include the national bestseller *A is for America: An American Alphabet* and *Memoirs of a Goldfish*. Devin lives in Michigan and anchors the news for WDIV-TV in Detroit.

Chris Ellison has illustrated both children's picture books and adult fiction for nearly 20 years. His books include *The Lucky Star* and *Let Them Play* (a 2006 Notable Social Studies Trade Book for Young People). Chris lives in Mississippi.

Doris Ettlinger graduated from the Rhode Island School of Design and has numerous picture books to her credit, including the award-winning *The Orange Shoes* and *Welcome to America, Champ!* Doris lives and teaches in western New Jersey.